Jennie Redbird Finds Her Friends

Jennie Redbird
Finds
Her Friends

Written by
Biloine W. Young
and Mary Wilson
Illustrated by Anne Samson

ISBN 0-8309-0087-X

Printed in the United States of America

Jennie Redbird Finds Her Friends

This is Jennie Redbird. Redbird is an Indian name and Jennie is an Indian girl. Jennie has black hair that her mother braids into two ponytails and ties with two blue ribbons. Jennie has big brown eyes and a wide happy smile that no one has seen for a long time.

Jennie does not smile much anymore because she is lonely for her old home and her friends at Red Lake. It is not like Jennie to be lonely and not have any friends. In fact, this is the first time in her life she has ever felt this way. Ever since her family moved to the city from Red Lake, Jennie has been alone and sad.

Her new house in the city is larger than her home at Red Lake had been, and she has a room of her own and does not have to share it with her baby brother. But Jennie still likes her old home better. She thinks houses in the city are too close together. There isn't even enough room between them to play a good running game.

Nothing is as much fun for Jennie in the city as it had been in Red Lake. When Jennie went to the store in Red Lake the storekeeper, Mr. Lightfoot, always leaned over the counter and said, "Hello there, Jennie Redbird. Would you like a red lollypop? Tell your mother I have some nice fresh eggs for her." And Mr. Lightfoot always gave her a red lollypop and a green one for her little brother.

One evening in the city Jennie's mother sent her to the corner grocery store for some bread and milk and peanut butter for supper. When Jennie got to the store the storekeeper met her with a frown and said, "Hurry up, kid. I'm just closing up so tell me what you want." Jennie was so startled by his gruff voice that she forgot what her mother wanted and she turned and ran back home.

Jipper, Jennie's dog, did not like the city either. In Red Lake Jipper chased squirrels and swam in the lake and caught garter snakes. But the first day in the city Jipper ran out in the street, right in front of some cars.

"Come back, Jipper," Jennie's father called. "Come back." Jennie's father tried to explain to Jipper that he had to stay in the yard but Jipper just sat there with his tongue hanging out, looking at them. So Jennie's father went for a piece of rope.

"I'm sorry, Jipper. But we will have to tie you up until you learn to stay in the yard." And Jipper was tied to the clothesline in the backyard.

Poor Jipper. Jennie felt just like Jipper. Having to stay on a narrow sidewalk was almost as bad as being tied up. Where, oh where, thought Jennie, are the fields to run in? And Red Lake to splash in? And, worst of all, where are all the new friends I was going to have in the city?

Jennie had never felt so lonely in all her life. She felt like crying, except that that was not what a brave little Indian girl should do.

One day Jennie was standing alone on the sidewalk when she looked up to see another little girl riding toward her on her bike. The girl slowed down as she came near Jennie and when she got closer she stopped.

"Hello," said the girl.

"Hello," said Jennie.

"My name is Susie Johnson. I live on the corner."

"I'm Jennie Redbird. I live right here."

"I know. We saw you move in. Do you like it here?"

Jennie was about to say "No," but she thought that wouldn't sound very polite. Besides, if she could have a friend like Susie, maybe she **would** like it. So she nodded and smiled and Susie smiled back.

"Would you like to ride my two-wheeler?" asked Susie. Jennie looked at the shiny bike Susie offered and shook her head. There had been no sidewalks where she lived on the reservation at Red Lake and she had never had a bike.

"I don't know how to ride—not yet," she said.

"Oh, that's too bad," said Susie. And she hopped on her bike and rode off to find someone else who could ride bikes with her.

Jennie felt like running back into her house and hiding, but that would not have been very brave. So instead she started walking down the sidewalk until she came to a park. Some boys were running and chasing each other in the park. Jennie stopped to watch. One of the boys smiled and waved to her.

"What are you playing?" she asked the smiling boy when he ran past.

"Cowboys and Indians," he said. "Do you want to play?"

"Oh, yes," said Jennie. "I'll be an Indian."

"You don't want to be that," said the boy. "You'll be chased and pushed down. You can be one of my cowboys."

"But I **am** an Indian," answered Jennie.

"Who cares?" said the boy. "It's still more fun to be a cowboy."

Jennie watched the boys chasing each other for a few more minutes and then turned back toward home. "I guess I won't play," she said, feeling more alone than ever.

When school started Jennie thought that now, at last, she would find some friends and not be lonely anymore. Jennie had loved her school at Red Lake. It had three rooms and a tiny kitchen where the teachers made coffee. The teacher knew all of the children and all of their mothers and fathers, too. The children brought their lunches in paper bags and the teachers would sit and talk and drink their coffee with the children during lunchtime.

Jennie's new school in the city was so big that she got lost the first two days. She did not know how to buy a lunch ticket and would have gone hungry if a teacher had not noticed and bought a lunch for her.

The first time she went to the cafeteria she did not know what to do and so she just walked through the food line without taking anything. A teacher had to lead her back a second time and show her the big stack of trays and the silverware in a napkin. It was hard for Jennie to understand that she was to take some of everything, but she did, even when the food looked strange and different.

One afternoon Jennie was sitting at a table looking at a book about Indians. The book had color pic-
tures of a big fight. The Indian men were wearing war
paint and were waving tomahawks over the heads of
the women and children. Behind some trees stood men
with long rifles aiming at the Indians. The people in
the book looked frightened of the Indians. Jennie was
frightened, too. They did not look like any of the Indians she knew, certainly not like her uncles or her
grandfather.

Maybe, thought Jennie, closing the book, maybe
I shouldn't tell anyone that I'm an Indian.

One morning, just before Thanksgiving, the teacher told the class they were to go on a field trip. That was another word Jennie did not understand. She knew what a **field** was and a **trip,** but what was a **field trip?** The other children were happy about going, so Jennie acted happy too.

The field trip was to a museum. The children were all lined up, two by two, with partners, to walk through the museum. Jennie walked into a big room with her class and looked up at a scene and, suddenly, she felt just as if she were back on the reservation. There, right in front of her, was Red Lake. And a woman just like her grandmother was cooking wild rice. In back was a canoe with a man gathering wild rice. And another figure, like her uncle, was getting ready to dance. One foot was raised, ready to start.

"Can anyone tell us what the people in this scene are doing?" asked the teacher. No one said a word. Jennie looked around. Didn't these children, who knew all about bicycles and cafeterias and field trips, know what this was?

"Jennie, can you tell us?" asked the teacher.

"They are gathering rice at Red Lake," said Jennie. "That's a man beating rice into his canoe. And the woman is cooking it and the dancer is . . ."

Jennie stopped talking. All the children had turned around and were looking at her. And they were smiling.

"Those are Chippewa Indians on Red Lake Reservation," said Jennie pointing to the scene in the museum. A big smile lit up her face. "And I'm a Chippewa, too," she said.

A few days later Jennie's class held an Indian powwow. Jennie's mother brought some of her Indian clothes so the class could trace them on brown paper. Everyone made headbands to wear. Jennie's father came in the afternoon to tell the class how he beat the wild rice into his canoe, and Jennie's mother cooked some rice right there in the room. All the children said it tasted good.

At the end of the powwow they danced. Jennie showed the class the steps and she beat the drum to get the rhythm just right. DUM dum dum dum, DUM dum dum dum. At first only the children danced. But then Jennie's mother came in wearing her beaded Indian clothes and took Susie's hand and began to dance. Then the teacher got up. The principal, walking down the hall, looked in the door and he began to dance too. It seemed to Jennie that the whole world was happy and dancing the Indian dances. The children looked at Jennie with shining eyes and, beating her drum, Jennie knew that she would not be lonely anymore.